MR. MESSY™

by Roger Hargreaves

Copyright© 1972, 1980 Roger Hargreaves
Published in U.S.A. by Price/Stern/Sloan Publishers, Inc.
410 North La Cienega Boulevard
Los Angeles, California 90048
Printed in U.S.A. All Rights Reserved.

ISBN: 0-8431-0812-6

PRICE/STERN/SLOAN
Publishers, Inc., Los Angeles
1983

Mr. Messy was the messiest person you've ever met in your whole life.

He lived in a particularly messy looking house.

The paint was peeling.

The windows were broken.

The garden gate was off its hinges.

And had Mr. Messy cut the grass in his garden lately?

He had not!

One morning Mr. Messy woke up in his messy bed, yawned, scratched, got up, brushed his teeth (leaving the top off the toothpaste), had his breakfast (spilling cornflakes all over the floor), and then set out for a walk (tripping over a broom he'd left lying in the garden two weeks before).

Mr. Messy walked through the woods behind his house.

He walked and walked right through the woods until he came to the other side.

And do you know what he found?

Mr. Messy found the neatest looking little cottage that he had ever seen.

There was a man in the garden, clipping the hedge.

He looked up as Mr. Messy approached.

"Good morning! I'm Mr. Messy!" said Mr. Messy.

"I can see that," replied the man looking him up and down. "I'm Mr. Tidy."

"And I'm Mr. Neat," said another man.

"Tidy and Neat," said Mr. Tidy.

"Neat and Tidy," said Mr. Neat.

"We're in business together," explained Mr. Tidy. "The people who own this house have asked us to do some work for them."

"What sort of work?" asked Mr. Messy.

"Oh, we make things nice and neat," said Mr. Neat.

"Perhaps we could come along and do some work for you?" said Mr. Tidy looking at Mr. Messy.

"But I don't want things neat and tidy," said Mr. Messy.

"Nonsense!" said Mr. Tidy.

"Fiddlesticks!" said Mr. Neat.

"But," said Mr. Messy.

"Come along," said Mr. Neat.

"Off we go," said Mr. Tidy.

"But, but . . . " said Mr. Messy.

"But nothing," said Mr. Neat, and off they all went to Mr. Messy's house at the other side of the woods.

"Good heavens!" said Mr. Neat when he saw where Mr. Messy lived.

"Good gracious me," added Mr. Tidy.

"This is the messiest house I have ever seen in all my born days," they both said at the same time.

"Better do something about it," said Mr. Neat.

Before Mr. Messy could open his mouth, the two of them were rushing about Mr. Messy's house.

Then they both went inside the house.

"Good heavens," said Mr. Neat.

"Good gracious," said Mr. Tidy.

And they set about cleaning the house from top to bottom.

They brushed and swept and polished and scrubbed and made the inside of the house look neater and tidier than it had ever looked before.

"There we are," said Mr. Tidy.

"All finished," said Mr. Neat.

"Tidy and neat," said Mr. Tidy.

"Neat and tidy," said Mr. Neat.

Mr. Messy just didn't know what to say.

Then they both looked at Mr. Messy.

"Are you thinking what I'm thinking?" Mr. Neat said to Mr. Tidy.

"Precisely," said Mr. Tidy.

"What we're both thinking," they said together to Mr. Messy, "is that you look much too messy to live in a neat and tidy house like this!"

"But . . . " said Mr. Messy.

But whatever Mr. Messy said was no use, and Mr. Neat and Mr. Tidy whisked him off to the bathroom upstairs.

Then Mr. Neat got hold of one of Mr. Messy's arms, and Mr. Tidy got hold of the other arm, and they picked him up and put him right into the bathtub.

Mr. Messy wasn't used to taking baths!

Mr. Neat and Mr. Tidy washed and brushed and cleaned and scrubbed and combed Mr. Messy until he didn't look like Mr. Messy at all.

In fact, he looked the opposite of messy!

He looked at himself in the mirror.

"You know what I'm going to have to do now?" he said in a rather fierce voice.

Mr. Neat and Mr. Tidy looked worried.

"What are you going to have to do?" they asked Mr. Messy.

"I'm going to have to change my name!" he said.

And then they all laughed together, and became the best of friends.

And that really is the end of the story except to say that if you're a messy sort of person you might have a visit from two people.

And you know what they are called, don't you?